Written & Illustrated
By
Kara "Picante" Muir

www.theadventuresofkarapicante.com

Published by Biggy Sancho Books, an imprint of Bench Press

ISBN 978-1-7349346-3-2 (ebook)
ISBN 978-1-7349346-2-5 (print)

For those who love pugs
and beavers
and pugs who love beavers.

"I am enough of an artist to
draw freely upon my imagination.
Imagination is more important
than knowledge.
Knowledge is limited.
Imagination encircles the world."
--Albert Einstein

Fiona was a dog. She was a fawn pug. (Fawn means: A color or pigment varying around a light grey-brown color.)

Fiona was full of mischief.

FIONA

Though Fiona was a dog
her people loved her
like a child.
One day Fiona's Girl-Person,
known as "Mama" in puggish
(the official language
of her breed),
brought her a present:

A stuffed, furry, squishy, squeaky beaver.
Mama threw the beaver and Fiona ran to fetch it.

Fiona played tug-of-war
with her beaver.

Fiona threw her beaver
up in the air
and tried to catch it.

Fiona napped with her beaver.

Fiona went to the
park with her beaver.

Fiona let other dogs smell
and chew on her beaver!

Fiona took her beaver
to faraway places.

And at the end of the day
Fiona went to bed
with her wet, bedraggled,
stuffed, furry, squishy, squeaky beaver...
And she dreamed.

What do YOU think Fiona dreamed about?

One day Fiona woke up
and her beaver was...
GONE!
Fiona looked everywhere
for her beaver.

Fiona looked under
her people's bed...
No beaver.

Fiona looked under the kitchen table...
No beaver.

Fiona ate a fly
and continued to look for her beaver.

Finally a distraught (which means "deeply agitated")
Fiona lay in her bed and longed for her
bedraggled, stuffed, furry, squishy, squeaky
and beloved beaver.

Meanwhile a thumping could be heard from the laundry room...
But Fiona continued to doze fitfully and fretfully,
tossing, turning and longing for her beaver.

Until she was roused from sleep by her mama,
who held Fiona's beaver in her hand.
It smelled brand new!

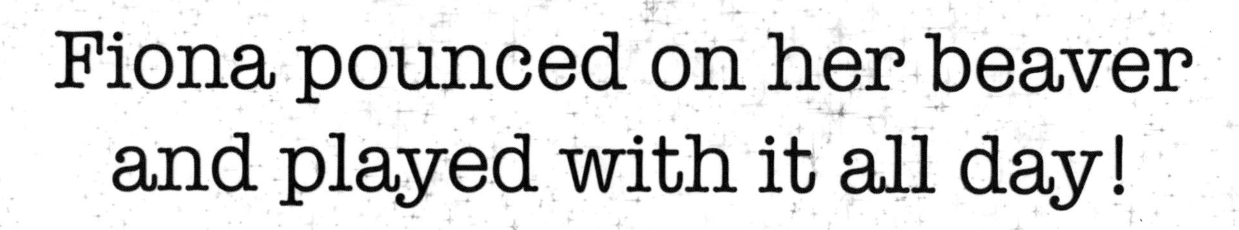

Fiona pounced on her beaver
and played with it all day!

Until once again her stuffed, squeaky and squishy
beaver was wet, stinky and bedraggled,
just the way Fiona liked it.
Soon she drifted off to sleep...

And she dreamed.

Kara "Picante" Muir is a massage therapist, craft artist/illustrator , blogger, belly dancer, and competitive air guitarist (tied for 4th best in 2019). She originally published "Fiona Plays With Her Beaver" in 2011 under the pen name "Morocco Leonard." After being diagnosed with stage 4 colorectal cancer in 2019, she started drawing pet portraits and eventually decided to re-illustrate her story of a pug and her beloved stuffed beaver. A native Oregonian, she lives in Portland with her husband and three dogs: Ruby Sue, Cooper, and Fiona, of course.

www.theadventuresofkarapicante.com

Acknowledgements

I would like to thank my beautiful husband Charles for believing in me and always encouraging me to be an idiot in the best ways.

To my cancer team at Providence Glisan Franz Cancer Center as well as my home health nurses, your kindness helps the medicine work. Thank you for assisting me to feel better.

To my massage clients who mean much more to me than that word conveys.

So much love to my air guitar family and "Team Picante," your encouragement and support has been invaluable to me. I will continue to strive to be worthy of it.
You make me humble.

An extra thank you to:
Jason & Lisa Farnan
Jennifer Pliska
Rob Messel
Claudia Andrews
Corrina Porterfield
Tatiana Sakurai
Tracy Boggs
Hillary Ryan
Jann & Gary Toole
Judith Boothby
David Tircuit
Amanda Latin
Marquina Iliev-Piselli
Kathy Seeley
Clark Conzatti
Deanna Reed
Kristiana Kroneck
Ziggy Hoyer
Sweetpea Rangel
Michelle Gilpin
Paula Lowden
Betsy Jones
Jeanna Redman
John & Jessica Dover
Mark Muir
Iggy Sancho
Megan Taylor
I have so much gratitude.
Thank you again, you people make it really hard not to stick around.

CPSIA information can be obtained
at www.ICGtesting.com
Printed in the USA
LVRC022330241120
672636LV00013B/65